Hensley Henson

Cui Bono?

an open letter to Lord Halifax on the present crisis in the Church of

England

Hensley Henson

Cui Bono?
an open letter to Lord Halifax on the present crisis in the Church of England

ISBN/EAN: 9783337381424

Printed in Europe, USA, Canada, Australia, Japan

Cover: Foto ©Andreas Hilbeck / pixelio.de

More available books at **www.hansebooks.com**

CUI BONO?

AN OPEN LETTER TO LORD HALIFAX

ON THE

Present Crisis in the Church of England.

BY

H. HENSLEY HENSON, B.D.,*

FELLOW OF ALL SOULS' COLLEGE, OXFORD,
INCUMBENT OF S. MARY'S HOSPITAL, ILFORD,
CHAPLAIN TO THE LORD BISHOP OF S. ALBAN'S,
RURAL DEAN OF SOUTH BARKING.

LONDON:

SKEFFINGTON & SON, PICCADILLY, W.

Publishers to H.M. the Queen and to H.R.H. the Prince of Wales.

1898.

—

(Price One Shilling.)

CUI BONO?

My Lord,

Little more than three years have elapsed since the Church of England exulted in a great electoral triumph. The Nation had spoken its mind in no uncertain tones, and that mind was decisively adverse to the policy of Disestablishment. On all hands men of affairs were heard to declare that the question had been laid to rest for a generation at least. To-day Disestablishment is on many men's tongues, and in all men's minds. The Leader of the Liberal Opposition seems half disposed to risk again, and on a greater scale, the experiment which wrecked his party in 1895. The Liberation Society exhibits once more its baleful activity. The " Free Churches " gather eagerly to another and more hopeful onslaught on their hereditary foe. Where yesterday all was dejection and perplexity, to-day there are all the signs of ardour and purpose. A transformation, equally surprising and melancholy, has passed over the political landscape. The victors of 1895 talk with apprehension and uncertainty : the vanquished never exulted in fairer chances. Nor is this all. The change has gone deeper. Grave Churchmen, to whom the idea of Disestablishment has been abhorrent, and who have hitherto rejected the very suggestion of Dis-endowment as a manifest impiety, are now discussing the necessity of the one, and the conditions of the other. A section of the clergy, neither numerically small nor personally insignificant, openly declares that in the destruction of the State connexion lies its best prospect of obtaining satisfaction for aims, which—whatever may be thought of their character—are held with passionate devotion and advocated with unflagging zeal. All this— so sudden and so ominous—compels reflection even in the most thoughtless. The question forces itself on the mind, and presses for answer, What has brought about this swift and tremendous revolution in the political outlook of the National Church? What is the spring from which consequences of such magnitude have flowed? The squalid agitation, set on foot by an obscure London fanatic, destitute of every claim to the public notice, has been the immediate antecedent, but assuredly not the ultimate cause. *That* lies deeper, and will operate when the iconoclasm of Mr. John Kensit has run its course. The agitation has uncovered the shrouded weakness of the National Church; it has forced into view the inveterate antagonisms within her pale : it has dragged into publicity aspects and tendencies of her manifold activity which are equally novel and repellent to the mass of Englishmen. The question has to be faced by every Churchman what attitude he shall adopt towards the sudden and imperative movement for a restoration of uniformity in the National Church. Shall he lend his influence to swell the demand for repressive legislation against the Ritualists? or shall he make a bold fight for the illegal or non-legal practices which impunity has made habitual in many congregations? or, finally, shall he cast in his lot with the ancestral enemies of the Church of England, and give his vote for Disestablishment and Disendowment? The situation is so grave and so difficult that no thoughtful Churchman can avoid a certain anxiety lest, in the inevitable excitement of an agitation conducted with a brutality happily of rare occurrence in English politics, partisan passions shall become exasperated beyond endurance, and the abiding interests of the Nation be sacrificed to the fury of domestic strife. In venturing to address to your Lordship a few reflections on the present state of the Church of England, I ought, perhaps, to justify my adoption of this mode of discussing a public question. I shall, however, content myself with two statements. I write an " Open Letter " because I desire to address myself to the mass of thoughtful English Churchmen, and they are not easily reached from the pulpit or the platform. I take the liberty of connecting my letter with your Lordship's name, because, not only are you recognized as the leader of a large section of the High Church Party, but also because you have indicated, by proposing a Conference, your own desire for the restoration of peace. In that desire I most sincerely concur, and my single object in writing is to minister to that blessed end. The mischiefs of the present agitation are, indeed, but too evident. A truly fearful responsibility rests on those who began, and on those who assist it. The fell and violent passions of the multitude have been deliberately excited, and the objects of their derision and even of their brutality have been very solemn religious facts. The clergy have been, are still, held up to public ridicule and detestation. Their sacred character has been dragged in the mire of popular scorn, and their access to many hearts wholly closed. Religion, itself, in becoming the subject of coarse jests and fanatical diatribes has largely lost its authority over large sections of the people. But I need not continue; the evil consequences of the present agitation are too plain to be missed by any, save the agitators themselves, to whom, indeed, it has brought notoriety, influence, and, in some cases, even pecuniary profit. I believe the greatest part of Churchmen would welcome an escape from the present confusion, and, certainly, the kindly reception accorded to your Lordship's suggestion of a Conference indicates as much. Personally, I cannot

profess myself very sanguine of the success of that method
of reaching harmony. It seems to be the first condition
of a useful Conference that the members should be agreed
on first principles, and, at least, generally on the objects
in view. Assuredly it would be extravagant to claim that
this condition would be fulfilled in any Conference which
was really representative of the English Church. Moreover, I cannot conceal from your Lordship that I feel a
certain resentment against private methods of dealing
with National questions. The Church of England does
not exist for the sake of the religious parties which play
so prominent a rôle in her history, nor can she permit
their interests to be identified with her own, or accept
their concordats as the law of her own being. Before
accepting the proposal of a Conference I should require to
be satisfied that it was adequately representative, that the
real issues would be placed before it, that its decisions
should be submitted to the ratification or rejection of the
Church at large. At present, indeed, I cannot perceive
such a measure of fundamental agreement and mutual
understanding as would justify any reasonable expectation
that a Conference would have any other result than to
still further embitter those who are now ranged in conflict. The imperative necessity of the hour is the discovery
of a common platform on which Church questions can be
discussed on their merits. As things now stand both the
contending parties appear to have adopted positions which
do not permit of any such discussion. The problems of
the National Church are regarded from standpoints so
arbitrary and so distinct that agreement is altogether
impossible. It is far from my present purpose to criticize
harshly any legitimate views of the English Church ;
I admit in advance that much may be true, and
much more be arguable, which yet cannot be accepted
in a useful discussion of practical difficulties. I

certainly hold that the National Church must comprehend within her fellowship widely divergent opinions, and, within certain inevitable limits, widely divergent practices; but this comprehension is only possible, and surely it is only reasonable on the condition of a generous mutual toleration. Standpoints which are legitimate enough for all the purposes of personal religion become intolerable when pressed as the necessary assumptions of public policy. Moreover, I must frankly say that neither the High Church nor the Low Church parties exhibit a very coherent or logical faith in their respective principles. Both profess principles which they cannot apply in practice, and which they would not if they could. In both cases the principles are for certain purposes, and under certain conditions true and serviceable; but in neither case are they so absolutely and universally true as to justify the passionate insistence which both parties equally manifest. The "undivided Church" and the "Reformation" are the opposing battle-cries; but if examined, neither the one nor the other can rightly be proposed as the final authority in the settlement of modern Church problems.

Apart from all questions of ecclesiastical theory, and considering only the practical worth of that authority of the "undivided Church" to which High Churchmen so frequently and so confidently appeal, can it be denied that we are little helped by an authority which is really unconscious of modern conditions, and wholly silent on many subjects of modern perplexity? I suppose the weightiest decisions of the "undivided Church" are enshrined in the canons of those famous "Œcumenical" Synods, to which the Church in all succeeding times has ascribed exceptional authority. But will the puzzled English Churchman be anywise assisted by a reference to those venerated decrees? Take the first and greatest of the Councils. Of the twenty genuine Canons of Nicæa [A.D. 325], not one (unless it be the first, which deals with a matter of no practical importance in modern times) is now fully observed; most are patently obsolete; and some, by the general procedure of the modern Church, are frankly disregarded. I am not aware that any later Council has specifically repealed the following rules, which, on the High Church theory, are binding on the modern Christian by the Divinest terrestrial authority of which we have knowledge :—

CANON III.—" The great Synod strictly forbids Bishops, Priests, and Deacons, and all clergymen, to retain any woman in their houses, under pretence of her being a disciple to them [συνείσακτον ἔχειν] ; but only a mother, sister, aunt, or other unsuspected person.

CANON XV.—" For the taking away the custom which prevails in some places contrary to Canon, it is decreed, on account of disturbances and disputes that have occurred, that neither Bishop, Priest, nor Deacon, remove from city to city : and that if anyone after the decree of the holy and great Synod attempt it, all the proceedings in this case shall be null, and the party shall be restored to the Church in which he was ordained.

CANON XX.—" Because there are some who kneel on the Lord's Day, and even in the days of Pentecost; that all things may be uniformly performed in every parish, it seems good to the holy Synod that prayers be made to God standing."

The Canons of Constantinople (A.D. 381), Ephesus (A.D. 431), and Chalcedon (A.D. 451) have reference, for the most part, to contemporary problems, and are wholly obsolete. I need not remind you that the Canons of these famous Synods form but a small part of the mass of ecclesiastical law which was recognized by the primitive

Church. The first Canon of Chalcedon expressly confirms "the Canons of the holy Fathers made in every Synod to this present time," language which Dr. Bright explains to include not only the decisions of Nicæa, Constantinople, and Ephesus, but those also "of the local Eastern Synods of Ancyra, Neocæsarea, Antioch, Gangra, and Laodicea." He adds that "when the Council of Chalcedon assembled, a collection of such Canons was current." Nor can the legislative legacy of the "undivided Church" be limited to the formidable mass of Canons recognized at Chalcedon : two, or, as the Easterns affirm, three more Œcumenical Councils passed fresh enactments : other Synods, less authoritative in themselves, were raised to œcumenical authority by the subsequent acceptance of their decrees. It would be an easy task to fill these pages with examples of Church Laws, which have never been repealed, because, since the division of East and West, no authority exists in the world competent to revise or repeal them, but which are obsolete, or impracticable, or contrary to modern conceptions of right, or based on demonstrable errors.

It may, however, be objected that no instructed "High Churchman" could be guilty of the patent absurdity involved in the view of œcumenical authority which I have criticized. The view of Catholic obligation, which is now in the ascendant, has cast aside the rigidity of the older Anglican doctrine, and inclines to accept as binding on the Church only so much of the primitive system as was incorporated in the tradition of the Western Church. The early Tractarians took a sterner view of their responsibility ; and the sixth Tract in their famous series was devoted to the task of proving "the present obligation of primitive practice." If I understand rightly your Lordship's language at Bradford, you are ready to acquiesce in the extensive departures from the primitive system which,

after the breach of ecclesiastical unity, took place in the
West. Protracted disuse of primitive practices amounts
in your opinion to a tacit, but not on that account the less
authoritative, repeal of conciliar decrees which had behind
them the weight of Catholic Antiquity. You recognize
the binding character of the Western revision of Primitive
Practice : subject, however, to yet one further limitation.
The " Book of Common Prayer " is allowed to supersede,
revise, and condemn the Western revision of Primitive
Practice. Your language was unambiguous and decisive :—

" We shall oppose by every means in our power any
" attempt to deprive us of the use of all such ceremonies,
" laudable customs, and practices not expressly forbidden
" by the Book of Common Prayer, with which the Church
" in the West has been used to accompany the Celebration
" of the Holy Eucharist."

Of course the authority of the Prayer-book is precisely
determined by its origin. I assume that your Lordship
accepts it as the formal and constitutional expression of
the mind of the National Church. The sanction of Convocation can hardly mean less than that, and such
sanction the Prayer-book does unquestionably possess.
I conclude, therefore, that the " High Church " party as
represented by your Lordship does really recognize the
plenary authority of the National Church to revise the
practical system of Primitive Catholicism, that the
precedents of the " undivided Church " may be lawfully
set aside by the English Convocation, and that in all
matters not affecting the faith and constitution of the
Church there is complete liberty of action vested in that
assembly. You, my Lord, are prepared to loyally
endorse the doctrine of the 34th Article.

" It is not necessary that Traditions and Ceremonies
" be in all places one, or utterly like ; for at all times
" they have been divers, and may be changed according to

"the diversities of countries, times, and men's manners,
"so that nothing be ordained against God's Word. . . .

" Every particular or national Church hath authority
" to ordain, change, and abolish, ceremonies or rites of
"the Church ordained only by man's authority, so that all
"things be done to edifying."

It seems to be clear that the constant references to the
"undivided Church" are superfluous and misleading.
That authority has long since been superseded, first by
the Western Church which built up a tradition of its own,
next by the National Church of England which revised,
superseded, and largely repudiated that tradition. That
the drastic action of the Reformers was avowedly determined by their preference for the discarded primitive
system may be admitted ; it does not affect the argument.
Western tradition or primitive practice are, even on the
High Church theory, only so far obligatory on the English
Churchman as they are not specifically set aside by the
law of the National Church. Neither the one nor the
other has any independent authority. The assent of the
National Church, either by positive enactment or by tacit
acceptance, is the condition of the recognition of that
authority : but, that condition fulfilled, the religious duty
of such recognition follows as a matter of course.

Now leaving outside the discussion all question of the
intrinsic reasonableness of this position, I am here concerned to show that in practice it is really destitute of
value. I need not travel beyond your Lordship's Bradford
speech for proof of this. You were dealing with the
practice of reserving the consecrated Elements for ministra-
tion to the sick. You asserted with justice that the
practice was primitive, and under certain circumstances
plainly convenient : and, then, you faced the Prayer-book.
The Bishop of Lichfield's dictum that reservation is
primitive but illegal you swept aside with some signs of

impatience : and you applied yourself to the task of dis-
proving what you disapproved. You explained away the
Rubric at the end of the Communion Service, and the
very decisive language of the 28th Article : you appealed
to the Dean of Lichfield against his Bishop, to a fourteenth
century constitution of Archbishop Peckham (which is
totally irrelevant if your main contention be unsound),
and, finally, to the Episcopate, not to settle the question
of interpretation between your Lordship and Bishop
Legge, but " in view of the necessities of the case and the
custom of the whole Church from the earliest times " to
" openly recognize " reservation. But you left out of
your argument a fact which, on your own principles, is
decisive of the whole issue. The Prayer-book has not
left the treatment of sick communicants in any uncertainty.
Even allowing (though, I think, few impartial men would
concede so much) that neither the Rubric in the Communion Service nor the 28th Article bear the sense they
seem to bear, and have been generally supposed to bear,
the illegality of reservation is beyond all question determined by the provision actually made for the Communion
of the Sick. Unprimitive certainly, inconvenient very
probably that provision may be, but there it is in plainest
enactment :—

  " But if the sick person be not able to come to the
" Church, and yet is desirous to receive the Communion in
" his house ; then he must give timely notice to the
" Curate, signifying also how many there are to com-
" municate with him (which shall be three or two at the
" least), and having a convenient place in the sick man's
" house, with all things necessary so prepared, that the
" Curate may reverently minister, he shall there celebrate
" the Holy Communion."

  My Lord, I submit that when the Prayer-book prescribes
a certain method of performing any Christian function,

that prescription is necessarily a prohibition of any other method. In this matter I am personally disposed to agree with your Lordship that the primitive system is preferable to that prescribed in the Prayer-book, but as to the prescription there is no possibility of doubt, nor as to the legal effect of it, nor as to the logical requirement of the theory which elsewhere you have affirmed. Here I may be permitted to point out that your Lordship stands committed to a very strict view of the obligation of Prayer-book Rubrics. You denounce in terms of great severity the clergy who omit to read the daily Offices, though the Rubric expressly refers that duty to their own judgment; or fail to celebrate the Holy Communion every Sunday and Saint's Day, though the Rubric expressly makes that rule contingent on a circumstance which in many parishes cannot always be counted on. Why does the Rubric for Communicating the Sick receive such scanty notice, or rather, why is it ignored altogether, when other Rubrics, dealing with matters of less gravity, are pressed so rigorously? Is it not evident that, whatever value for other purposes your view of Authority may have, for the purpose of a serviceable discussion of practical problems it is useless? Can it be altogether condemned as unreasonable or unfair that ordinary Englishmen, unversed in the subtleties of ecclesiastical theory, should conclude that your Lordship, and those whom you represent, recognize the binding force of the Rubrics only so far as they coincide with their own pre-conceived notions, and ignore Rubrics without hesitation when they conflict with those notions? Would it not be more frank and more practically useful to abandon these misleading appeals to the "undivided Church," and "the Church of the West," and the Prayer-book, as if any of these or all of them together were adequate for the guidance of the Church in her treatment of the problems, unsuspected in

earlier times, of modern life? It is no disrespect to these
venerable Authorities, nor does it argue any unwillingness
to accept the guidance of the past, to maintain that present
experience also has its rightful claim, and that the law of
progress in Religion as in every other sphere is necessarily
a law of change? I plead for a discussion of our religious
difficulties which shall be frank, free, and fearless. A
conference in which the several members are pledged in
advance to certain decisions could lead to nothing but
exasperation. Your Lordship seems to concede this when
you remark with obvious justice "that the questions with
"which the Church of England has to deal cannot ade-
"quately be dealt with merely by a reference to the
"settlement of the fifteenth and sixteenth [? sixteenth and
"seventeenth] centuries": but you seem to recede again
into the confusion of your theory when you warn the
Bishops in a tone which is minatory to the verge of disrespect, "that if they would exact respect for their own
"authority, it can only be in proportion as they them-
"selves recognize and submit to the authority of that
"whole Catholic Church of Christ, of which the Church
"of England is but a part, to which it appeals, and to
"which the Episcopate, no less than the clergy and laity,
"are bound to submit." The suspicion crosses the mind
on reading such words that your Lordship does not really
concede to the National Church any true autonomy, not
of course in the sphere of the Faith, or the Sacraments,
or the Apostolic Ministry, which admittedly lie outside
the range of national action, but of discipline and worship
and ecclesiastical customs: and, further, it must be con-
ceded that the curious hostility to the term "Anglican"
which has manifested itself in the English Church Union,
of which your Lordship is the President, and which
inspired some amazing utterances at Bradford from a
well-known East End Incumbent, lends support to this

suspicion. Nevertheless, in the absence of any express declaration to the contrary, I prefer to believe that, since you are prepared to accept the Prayer-book modifications of the Western tradition with respect to the mode of Eucharistic Celebration, you are equally prepared to acknowledge the right of the same National Church, which put forward the Prayer-book, to exercise no diminished authority with respect to other matters.

If, leaving the High Church party, I turn to their opponents, I find that the same fault in a still more aggravated form marks their discussion of our practical difficulties. The " Reformation " is inscribed on the banners of agitators who would be distressed indeed to define the meaning of the phrase. It is, indeed, the mis-fortune of the Low Church party to have the support of the ignorant multitudes of the lower middle-class, whose religious prejudices are hereditary, and who seem, beyond all other sections of English folks, to be subject to night-mares of religious terror, or suspicion. It would, of course, be unjust to credit the party as a whole with the fanaticism of its rank and file, yet it cannot be denied that the pros-pects of a peaceful solution of the ecclesiastical problems of the hour are gravely compromised by the unreasoning and intractable attitude of the "Protestant" masses. The more moderate Low Churchmen profess to take their stand on the " Reformation Settlement," and they accept the Prayer-book as the authoritative declaration of that settle-ment. But not without large exceptions. They repudiate with some contempt a literal insistence on either the language of the formularies, or the practical directions of the rubrics. They, too—like their rivals—subscribe the Prayer-book with an *arrière pensée* to the effect that where it clashes with another authority (in this case the " Protestant Faith," in that the " Primitive Church " and the " Western tradition ") they will repudiate its doctrine and ignore its rules. If the interests concerned were not so serious, the aspect of these competitors in artifice would be actually ludicrous. The Prayer-book, in their hands, bears no inapt resemblance to the venerable relics of ancient Rome in the middle ages. The rival families of the city united to facilitate their decay by using them as a common quarry from which to obtain materials for their internecine conflicts. Both parties have their pet rubrics, which they themselves religiously obey, with which they confront one another, by which they vainly strive to prove their own loyalty and the dishonesty of their rivals. Neither accepts all the Rubrics, and, for the best of reasons, the Rubrics are not capable of practical application. Under these circumstances it would seem the obvious duty of sensible men to recognize that a reasonable course must lie in one of two directions. Either patient mutual tolerance, or revision of the Prayer-book ; a passionate insistence on unqualified obedience to the Prayer-book is indecent in those, who themselves habitually disobey some or other of its rules, and that is the case equally with High Churchmen and with Low Churchmen. To this subject I shall recur later.

I do not pursue the subject further here because my purpose is not to formally criticize the contending partisan theories, but to point out their practical insufficiency ; and, on that ground, to submit that, for our present necessities, it is futile to appeal against the existing system of the National Church to the law and practice of the undivided Church in the one case, or the " Reformation " in the other. I am far from denying the legitimacy or questioning the value of a constant reference to both. The experience of Christians, though gained under different conditions and in a long-distant age, can never be destitute of value. The problems

which confront the Church in her Divine Warfare are
at once always novel and always ancient. The circumstances of human life are in continual flux, and the positive
regulations which match the needs of one generation will
scarcely do as much for any other. It would seem the
primary condition of a sound judgment in ecclesiastical
affairs to distinguish clearly between principles which are
of perpetual validity, and institutions which at best have
but a contingent and temporary usefulness. The rigidity
of mental attitude revealed in the religious controversy
which has filled the columns of newspapers, both secular
and religious, and distracted the minds of men beyond
recent precedent, fills me with despondency. The
" Reformation " on the one side, and the " Undivided
Church" on the other have become mere shibboleths,
exasperating the minds of men, and really destitute of
any practical worth.

My Lord, while these " Shibboleths " are bandied to
and fro in the conflict of parties, the Church of England
stands to lose, whichever way the victory inclines. There
are, as I have already said, many signs that the general
body of citizens is growing resentful of these incessant
disputes, and tends to incline an attentive ear to the
suggestions of those, the ancestral foes of the English
Church, who counsel the ruinous policy of Disestablishment. I observe that the " High Church " party is growing
more patient of the prospect of Disestablishment, and not
a few of the more ardent members of the party openly
declare that they are looking in that direction for escape
from present difficulties. Their rivals are being forced by
the necessities of the agitation to which they have, in evil
hour, committed themselves, into an ever closer association
with the Nonconformists. That alliance has its price, and
that, acquiescence in the political project which the Nonconformists pursue with an almost religious ardour. The

moment is propitious for the advent of a destructive politician of ability : the National Church, torn with internal dissensions, invites attack : her normal enemies have been suddenly reinforced from unexpected quarters, and a great political party confessedly needs a policy which could quicken its enthusiasm and re-unite its ranks. It must be confessed that the ecclesiastical outlook is not encouraging. What can be the outcome of the amazing agitation which has spread sacrilege and blasphemy from one end of England to the other ? Some parliamentary action seems to be necessary, if English precedents are to hold good. What will that action be ? All men agree that it will be directed towards the restraint of Ritualism : whether that restraint be really required or not need not here be discussed. Probably the overwhelming majority of Churchmen are agreed that a stiffening of Authority against clerical individualism is required : nevertheless the passing of any Act in restraint of Ritualism would only intensify the existing anarchy. Experience has made it abundantly evident that the Ritualistic clergy are so wedded to the practices which they have adopted that no adverse laws would obtain their obedience. The familiar cycle of events would be duly rehearsed. The law passed amid the frenzied zeal of its promoters would be treated with ostentatious contempt by its victims. The dangerous and delusive cry of "Erastianism" would certainly be raised, and as certainly would rally to the party of resistance large numbers of excellent Churchmen, whose zeal for the Church's theoretical rights is unchastened by any adequate appreciation of facts. There might be prosecutions : in that case, there would be a new succession of "martyrs." The exasperation of parties would be extreme, and could hardly fail to create a general demand for Disestablishment from the High Church party. Such a demand would moralize the policy of the Liberation

Society, and go far to reconcile the national conscience to projects which in themselves are nefarious.

I venture, therefore, to make appeal to all who regard with fear and aversion the prospect of Disestablishment to weigh seriously the actual tendency of their own action at this juncture : and I add my protest against the perilous insistence on partisan positions which marks the attitude of the combatants on both sides of the present conflict.

I submit that the true and only legitimate standpoint from which to regard ecclesiastical questions is that of the religious interest of the nation. The Church of England is the principal instrument by means of which Christianity is brought to bear on the national life. I suppose even her political opponents will admit as much as this. The Nonconformist bodies are active, and, it is confidently affirmed, growing : undoubtedly they have exercised a powerful influence on English society, and in the main, though with considerable exceptions and limitations, that influence has been wholesome. But these denominations are all of recent growth, the most aggressive is of yesterday, and most have only become considerable within this century. They have no roots in antiquity : their development is rapid, but not more rapid than their decline : they produce few theologians of distinction, and their moral effect is seriously compromised by their inveterate political attachments. Moreover, they are not well adapted for pastoral work : they languish wherever the conditions of life are unfavourable to sensational methods. It would not be wholly unjust to say that their strength and their weakness lie in the fact that they tend to reflect contemporary social and political movements. Over great part of England they are practically unknown. The National Church in hundreds of country parishes, and in the poorest urban districts, is the sole representative to the people of the Faith and Discipline of Christ.

Disestablishment and disendowment would handicap, or
wholly extinguish, the ministrations of religion over great
part of the country. Nor would even this be the full
extent of the calamity. You, my Lord, will appreciate
the gravity of the failure of the National Schools. I
submit that nothing could avert that failure if the Church
were disestablished. The necessary extinction of numerous
country cures, the extreme poverty of the clergy, the loss
of prestige and even of legal position, the infinite disturb-
ance which would be caused by the process of disendowment, and the extreme exasperation of men's minds, would
inevitably—if anything in human affairs can be described
as inevitable—bring about the failure of the National
Schools, which have been sustained so long mainly by the
exertions and sacrifices of the clergy.

Hitherto I have assumed that the Church of England
would hold together through the process of Disestablishment, but I do not believe it. When I read the utterances
of the leaders on both sides of the present controversy, I
am amazed that even the generous latitude of a National
Church can embrace such conflicting opinions. If the
agitation now proceeding has done nothing else, it will at
least have demonstrated the immense value of the State
connexion as an instrument of ecclesiastical harmony.
What other power than that of the great National
Tradition could hold together antipathies so fierce,
aspirations so contradictory, methods so opposed!
Remove that power, and what remains to arrest the
natural movement of these heterogeneous elements?
Disestablishment means the release of centrifugal forces
which no homilies on Christian fellowship can charm
into quiescence. The National Church must face, in
the wake of humiliation and pillage, the last ignominy
of disruption. There are, perhaps, some persons who
can regard this prospect with equanimity; they would

prefer the liberty of denominationalism to the unity of
a National Institution; they would exchange the "honesty"
of avowedly opposed sects to the delusive harmony of an
established Church. I am not of this way of thinking.
To my mind religion gains in breadth of view and range
of influence infinitely more than it loses in ecclesiastical
symmetry and ardour of conviction by the fact of Establishment. I observe that while the latter qualities rarely
are lacking to Christendom, the former are always tending
to be lost. I do not think the quality of religion among
the disestablished and non-established denominations is
so superior to that among ourselves as to encourage
the desire for Disestablishment. Moreover, I see that
at present there is nothing more necessary to the interest
of English Christianity than breadth of view and range of
influence. The forces that normally tend to narrow the
sympathies and restrict the activity of religious people are
more than usually powerful ; such forces, I ,mean, as
reactionary panic, and controversy, and, perhaps, proselytizing zeal. The wisdom of the Church is to wait, to
avoid conclusions of disputed points, to mark time for
awhile before resuming progress. Establishment enables
this ; the very indignation with which the paralysis of the
National Church is denounced by Church Reformers, more
zealous than far-sighted, proves the restraining effect of
the State connexion. Our anomalous and even anarchic
state indicates that Anglican autonomy is not in working
order. The enemies of the Church of England are not
slow to make capital out of her apparently helpless condition. She seems to float on the national life like a
rudderless derelict. No doubt there is mischief and fault
in all this. It may be that we have been, as a Church,
too complacent, and that, in some directions where the
truth was apparent, we ought to have been more vigorous
in asserting rights which, though long dormant, are con-

stitutionally unimpeachable. But, allowing this, can it be denied that the Church of England has, on the whole, gained in breadth and spirituality by her legislative and disciplinary paralysis during this century, and that experience suggests that we have yet more to gain from the same harsh necessity? Has the Roman Church gained or lost by that legislative freedom, which the Church of England has temporarily lost? May it not have been a disguised blessing that, against our will and in spite of our legal rights, we, as a Church, have been preserved from precipitate conclusions on many matters which are not really ripe for treatment, though in any truly autonomous society they must have been made the subject of legislation? And ought we not to be very slow to accept the vehement counsels of the zealots of ecclesiastical theory when we see in our own experience how considerable indirect advantages may be involved in an ecclesiastical position which in theory is humiliating and indefensible? Now one of the first results of Disruption would be an outburst of legislative activity. The several fragments of the dismembered Church will hasten to realize their partisan conceptions. The Low Church party released from the widening influence of Catholic beliefs will shrivel into a narrow Protestantism; the High Church party, no longer held to evangelical connexions, will degenerate into an equally narrow Ritualism. The basal agreements which once had been kept in a salutary prominence must inevitably fall into the background, and the chief place be given henceforward to the doctrines and practices which are not basal, but distinctive of party. And this disaster will happen at a time when, throughout Christendom, the rift between educated thought and revealed religion is perceptibly widening. The broad tolerance of the Established Church has, hitherto, in England kept together in an exceptionally close union culture and the Christian profession ; but when that honourable quality has vanished with the conditions which made it possible, who can doubt that here also the disastrous breach will become visible, and Faith grow alienated from Science ? The process will be hastened, and, possibly, determined by a factor which cannot be ignored. The Roman Church is now strongly planted in this country, not assuredly in the hearts of the people, still less in their respect, but in their midst a highly organized army of invasion, fed from abroad. That Church has sacrificed every higher ideal to the single project of earthly dominion : proselytizing, in the bad sense which the word has come to bear, is the law of modern Romanism. Is it excessive to believe that the disruption of the Church of England would enormously benefit her most relentless antagonist ? We know how powerful an attraction is possessed by the Roman Church, and how strongly the fascination of her fellowship is even now felt by the "advanced" members of the High Church party ; is it not certain that when political disaster had been quickly followed by ecclesiastical disruption that attraction would be still more powerful, and that fascination still more alluring ?

You will say that these gloomy forebodings are, after all, largely speculative : that the event may falsify them. This may be allowed, but even so, I submit that they are extremely probable, and that in forming a judgment on a course of action reasonable men must reckon with those results as *certain* which are, on good grounds, seen to be *probable*. Two results of Disestablishment, however, are assured, and they alone might decide a reflective Churchman to oppose that project to the uttermost—on the one hand, an enormous financial strain would be brought to bear on all religious work ; on the other, a Marah stream of social bitterness would be set flowing in every parish.

The alienation of the ancient endowments, involving the loss of an annual income, which on the lowest estimate cannot be reckoned as less than £3,000,000, is no slight matter. The debasement of spiritual work by the financial straits of the clergy is even now a formidable and a grow-ing evil. I can speak with the authority of personal experience on this matter. The Church in the districts where it has been my fortune to labour is largely without endowment, living " from hand to mouth," after the ideal of " Voluntaryism." I do not hesitate to affirm that the moral and spiritual " cost of collection " is appalling. Does anyone who observes the current methods of obtain-ing money for religious and charitable objects doubt this ? Are not " bazaars " a proverb of spiritual degradation ? Is not philanthropic advertisement an organized system of sensationalism, not to say mendacity? Are not " statistics " of religious progress a by-word ? These things are ruinous to religion, however indispensable they may be to the maintenance of religious work. Can any reflective Churchman contemplate without alarm so vast an increase of all these evil things ? I confess I sometimes reckon the despiritualizing of the Church as one of the worst of the many evil promises of Disendowment. But even this is not the worst. Society will be cloven asunder by fierce resentments, which will not be assuaged for generations. In every parish there will be the bitterness of a great injury on one side, the arrogance of a baleful triumph on the other. The character of local politics, not very high at any time, will be irrecoverably ruined by the influx of the distracting animosities of a great religious feud. The best friends of local government have many reasons for regarding its future with apprehension : Dis-endowment will more than fulfil their gloomiest forecasts.

My Lord, I have written so largely on this matter because it is vital to my argument that the bearings of

Disestablishment on the religious interest of the English people should be clearly apprehended. In view of these grave probabilities I submit that it is our imperative duty as good Churchmen and (though the two characters cannot really be distinguished) as good citizens to exert ourselves by all legitimate methods to preserve inviolate the National Status and Heritage of the Church of England. I proceed to discuss the broad conditions on which, as I see the facts, on which alone that end can be secured.

I. If the Church of England is to remain an Established Church, her members must accept a large measure of Denominational Self-suppression. It is not sufficiently remembered that the denominational strength of the Church is enormously inferior to what her public services seem to require. Indeed, as a denomination, the Church is painfully, almost ridiculously insignificant, when compared not with the Nonconformist bodies, none of which can vie with her in numbers, but with the Nation itself which accepts and commissions her as its Spiritual Organ. Probably not one in thirteen of the Electors is a Communicant at her altars : certainly one-third, possibly one-half, of the professed Christians in the country, definitely repudiate her membership. The vast majority of the people live habitually in neglect of her ordinances. It is evident that she is in no position to adopt the masterful tone of those earlier times when she exercised spiritual authority over all, or nearly all the nation. She must found her claim to State Recognition not on her overwhelming denominational strength, but on her manifest services to the community. Her claim, thus founded, is a very strong one. For her denominational weakness gives no truthful indication of her general influence. The National Church bears on the national life in a thousand unsuspected ways. Her power is felt, and always felt for good, in many directions : perhaps her highest and most beneficent achievements are not capable of tabulation in the " Church Year Book." She lays restraining hand on the eager selfishness of a mercantile community : she mitigates by her untiring charity the inevitable hardships of a luxurious civilization : she chastens the pride of wealth, and cheers the desolation of poverty : across the yawning chasms which open between classes and interests she throws the holy connexions of her manifold and ubiquitous philanthropy. In the great urban parishes where not five per cent. of the population make any regular profession of Christianity, the clergy, by their pastoral labours, bring into the parochial life an element of kindliness and morality and hope, which is, viewed from the standpoint of the national interest, almost infinitely valuable. As they move about the streets on their accustomed duties, they are a perpetual protest against the squalid and hungry materialism of popular life, they incarnate before the roughest sections of our people the Moral Law, not as a coercive force, but as a general and ever-present Appeal to the Conscience, and their presence is felt as a rebuke to every form of baseness. In one populous and squalid parish which I know, the police on one occasion, when the force had to be largely withdrawn for concentration in another district, requested the parochial clergy to show themselves in the streets, as their mere presence would suffice to restrain serious disorder. Now these immense National Services do justify to the conscience of the Democracy the continued Establishment of the Church, in spite of the fact that, as a denomination, she is far too insignificant to claim a National recognition. But manifestly her tenure of the National Status involves a recognition on her side of the actual circumstances under which it is granted to her. The Church has had to learn by a series of sharp lessons that no privileges or exemptions can be implied in Establishment. In that sense Establishment has been finally condemned by the national conscience. Establishment remains to-day in an attenuated form, binding the Church to wider duties, conferring on the people large religious franchises, but conveying no privilege to the one, and inflicting no hardship on the other. If any grievances yet remain unredressed they need only be pointed out and substantiated by adequate proof, and their removal will be promptly effected. The State asks from the Church a large sacrifice of denominational liberty : it offers in return a splendid vantage-ground from which to wage her spiritual warfare. The Church has to choose between her own interest as a denomination, and the interest of her redemptive work. My Lord, I cannot doubt what is her duty : she carries the Name, and Commission, of Him Who in His own Person gave example of Self-suppression. On a memorable occasion the Evangelist relates that He checked very solemnly the ambition of the sons of Zebedee; His Words seem to me eminently needed by us all at the present time. " Jesus called them to Him, and saith unto "them, Ye know that they which are accounted to rule "over the Gentiles lord it over them ; and their great "ones exercise authority over them. But it is not so among "you: but whosoever would become great among you, shall "be your minister : and whosoever would be first among "you, shall be servant of all. For verily the Son of Man "came not to be ministered unto, but to minister, and to "give His life a ransom for many " (S. Mark xi. 42-5).

My Lord, you will not do me the injustice of supposing that I am unconscious that a point may be reached in the State's demand upon the Church, at which a higher interest than that of her immediate work would demand an assertion of her latent denominational rights : nor am I so arrogant as to assume that my own judgment ought to be accepted by anyone else as determining when that point is reached. Yet, with all deference, I would submit to your Lordship that, as things now stand in England, no one can maintain without extravagance that the State so limits the spiritual liberty of the Church as to make it the duty of Churchmen to seek release from Establishment. Let any thoughtful Churchman read the remarkable and most timely declarations in which the honoured Chief of the Church of England has recently set forth, in words of characteristic lucidity and a certain stately simplicity, the broad conditions of teaching and worship in the National Church, and let him ask himself in all gravity whether it be not monstrous to affirm that those conditions are either iniquitous in principle or intolerable in practice. For seven years I held a great parish, which the late Bishop of S. Alban's was wont to describe as the most difficult in his diocese, and which certainly did present an amazing variety of difficult problems. I was unquestionably, as Vicar of Barking, well placed for testing the working value of the Establishment : and I can honestly say that, though I ever loyally tried to obey the law, and have at no time had the slightest sympathy with clerical illegality, I did not find in the legal requirements of my position any hindrance to my spiritual work. Hindrances enough there were, and not least among them my own incapacity, but certainly it would be monstrous to affirm that the State hindered the Church. On the contrary, I found in the National Status which I received from the fact of Establishment a most valuable starting-point for spiritual work. It opened the doors of the parishioners to my visits ; it justified to their consciences my attempts to reform the more glaring iniquities of the local life ; it provided me with a common platform on which I could approach pastorally persons with whom I had otherwise no relation. I adduce my own experience, my Lord, because I am at least entitled to speak with authority on that subject, and because I desire, even at the risk of an imputation of egotism, to make plain the practical bearings of those vehement denunciations of the Establishment in which some Churchmen are but too ready to indulge.

II. If the Church of England is to remain an established Church the clergy must recover the popular confidence. It is a sad assumption that underlies this proposition, but it is undoubtedly true. The clergy have largely lost the confidence of the people. Into the causes of this unfortunate fact I cannot here enter at length. It must suffice to point out that they are long-standing, complex, and largely impersonal. The circumstances of the English Reformation were unparalleled elsewhere. Alone of the Reformed Churches the Church of England retained the ancient episcopal government unimpaired : but this advantage was not secured without a heavy sacrifice. Alone of the Reformed Churches the Church of England has never been popular, for she has never reflected the triumph of any dominant popular party. In Scotland, for example, the Presbyterian Church expressed and secured the national aspirations of the Scottish people. The Covenants symbolized not unworthily the actual fact. The Church is the creation of Scottish national feeling, and enshrines the patriotic traditions of a brave and high-spirited race. In England the last influence that can be recognized in the long and various process of "the Reformation" is the popular will. The Tudor despotism strove for the best part of a century to force an Anglican system on the nation, and failed. The weaker Stuarts, taking up the task under more difficult conditions and with inferior resources, brought the whole ecclesiastical constitution to violent disaster : and though, after the Restoration, the Church seemed for awhile to be deeply rooted in the popular favour, the Nonconformists remained a powerful factor. The Revolution of 1688 necessarily involved a frank recognition of Nonconformity; complete religious equality has, indeed, only been secured within the present century, but, in principle, the failure of political Anglicanism was admitted by the Toleration Act of 1689. The accession of the Hanoverian dynasty undoubtedly affected injuriously the interests of the National Church. How strained the relations between the clergy and the government became is sufficiently indicated by the thoroughly unconstitutional silencing of the Convocations for more than a century (1717-1852). The effect of all this was to impress the popular mind with a settled suspicion of the ecclesiastical character. I need hardly point out how potent an influence in the same direction has been exercised by the " Oxford Movement." Whatever opinion may be held as to the general character of the Tractarian agitation, no instructed and candid Churchman any longer questions the lofty ideals and the high personal sincerity of the authors and leaders, and few will deny that large benefits have, from that source, come to the Church and the Nation. There has, however, been this fatal defect in the whole movement. It was academic and clerical in its origin : in 1845 it ceased to be academic, and became more than ever clerical : and that is its character to this day. The laity have, in the main, been but little affected by the Tractarian movement. No doubt individuals here and there, and congregations in London and some of the greater provincial cities, have accepted Tractarian principles, but in the main it has not been so. The English Church Union, over which your Lordship presides, is pardonably proud of its numbers, and they are, from some points of view, impressive enough. I take them to illustrate my present contention. The total membership of the Union is stated to be 33,000, of whom

4,200 are clergymen (including 31 Bishops), and nearly 29,000 are lay communicants. I do not quite understand whether the 10,000 women associates are included in the membership, but, leaving them out of reckoning, what do the figures really prove, but this—that while one clergyman in every six is a High Churchman, only one layman in twenty can be so described? This, however, though not without significance, enormously overstates the strength of the High Church party : for the English Church Union only includes communicants, and the enormous majority of Englishmen are not included in that category. Melancholy though this must be by every good Churchman considered, yet it is not necessary to make it worse than experience proves it to be. For many reasons, the average law-abiding, clean-living Englishman, who attends the Parish Church Services, and readily supports any good work, is not easily persuaded to come to Holy Communion, but he is not an unbeliever, and must nọt be so reckoned. Such men, numbered by many hundreds of thousands, have no sympathy with the principles of Tractarianism. In any case 29,000 laymen above the age of sixteen form rather a petty force in a nation of which the Parliamentary electors alone exceed five millions. The effect of the Oxford movement has been to drive a wedge between the clergy and the people. The clergy are working and teaching on one conception of Christianity, the people are living and listening on another. The very phraseology of the two has become distinct. The Vicar speaks of the Holy Eucharist, the Altar, the priest, Catholicism, and so forth ; the Churchwarden of the Lord's Supper, the Table, the parson or minister, Protestantism, and the like. The relations of clergymen and parishioners become as " non-natural " as the exegesis of Tract 90. The development from "non-natural " to artificial and unreal is facile and swift. It is very clear that all the

conditions of mutual suspicion are here provided. But
this is by no means all. The High Church clergy have
ambitions which may be, and commonly are, in themselves
innocent and laudable, but which they dare not avow.
They believe in the spiritual value of Confession, for
instance, and they desire to promote that discipline among
their people : but they are afraid to openly say as much :
they seek their object quietly as occasion offers. Is it any
marvel that they are the objects of parochial suspicion ?
nay, do they not in part, at least, deserve the obloquy
they undoubtedly receive ?

Two facts in particular have damaged the reputation of
the clergy for honesty. The first is the secessions to
Rome. In 1845 and in 1851 on a great scale, commonly
on a very small one, High Church clergymen have seceded
to the communion which the English laity as a whole
regard with unreasoning abhorrence. Hardly a year passes
without some clerical secession. The fact is easily enough
explained, and the explanation is neither honourable to
Rome nor discreditable to the Church of England, but
one, and one only explanation suggests itself to " the man
in the street." He concludes that the seceding parson was
all along a Romanizing "conspirator." The other fact
is the ostentatious contempt of Law and Rubric which
many High Church clergymen *seem* to exhibit. I am not
ignorant, of course, that the most anarchic of the Ritualists
has explanations which at least in his own opinion ex-
onerate him from the guilt of disobeying the Law, but, it
must be allowed, that those explanations are not capable
of such simple statement as to reach the general understanding. It is far from my intention to prefer an indict-
ment against the Ritualist clergy : their apology may for
all I know be convincing and sufficient. I am only concerned to point out that it is unintelligible to the average
layman. He knows that the clergyman has solemnly

pledged himself at his Ordination to use the Prayer-book
and obey the Bishop, and he sees him manifestly altering
the familiar services almost beyond recognition, and quite
brazenly setting at naught the " fatherly admonitions " of
his Bishop. He neither knows, nor cares about the " First
Prayer-book," or the " Sarum use," or the subtle distinction
between "canonical " and other obedience, or the mys-
terious transmutation of the Court of Arches into a lay
court, or the spiritual insufficiency of the Judicial Com-
mittee, or a thousand other formulas and contentions
which fill the atmosphere of clerical assemblies. He has
the Prayer-book in his hand, and cannot find his way
about the service in many Churches by its once-sufficient
guidance. He respects the Law, and is really shocked that
his clergyman does not. Again, I ask, is it any marvel
that he grows restless and suspicious ? Is it right or
charitable to provoke his almost inevitable indignation ?
Ought we not rather to follow the Apostolic counsel and
" take thought for things honourable in the sight of all
men " ? My Lord, it would ill reflect the honesty I am
advocating if I stopped here. Your Lordship knows, and
I know, that there are some clergy who are in this sense
dishonourable men, that they are consciously and deliberately pursuing aims which they know to be contrary to
the whole drift and intention of the English Church. The
Bishops, with few exceptions, assure us that only a small
section of the clergy are positively disloyal. Their Lordships unquestionably have access to information which
other men cannot obtain : they speak with the double
authority of knowledge and responsibility. I cheerfully
accept their assurance, but I point out that the public
offence caused by disloyalty of this manifest and guilty
character is out of all proportion to the number of clergymen concerned. A general uneasiness is created which
spreads and deepens into that præternatural suspicion

which is the condition of every kind of injustice. The
reception accorded to Mr. Walsh's "Secret History of
the Oxford Movement" is full of ominous suggestion.
The mingled credulity and craft of the Author are infinitely
discreditable to himself—and the work is everywhere dis-
figured by insinuations of dishonourable conduct against
men, about whose nobility of character the Nation has
long since made up its mind : it is a bad book, and it has
a bad effect on the mind, but, in spite of all, it does
succeed in fastening on the High Church clergy the hateful
accusation of religious duplicity, and so raising against
them the ignorant but essentially righteous manliness of
average Englishmen. It is often asserted by way of
apology for the lawlessness of Ritualists that as a matter of
fact the Church owes her present ritual liberty to nothing
else. Even allowing this to be true, it is but too often
forgotten that the success of lawlessness is always very
dearly purchased. Ritual liberty is a poor exchange for
the confidence of the English people, and yet, nothing less
has been forfeited during the process of defying and dis-
crediting the law-courts. The reflective Churchman will
not regard with unmingled satisfaction any advantages
won at the cost of weakening in the general mind respect
for authority. Personally, I think the Church has lost
far more than she has gained by the policy of the
Ritualists. It is not sufficiently remembered that under
the conditions of modern life the vagaries of individuals
rapidly attract notice, and in exact proportion to their
extravagance is their notoriety. The constant movements
of population bring under the public view the extraordinary
variety of ritual in the National Church. There is some-
thing almost pathetic about the professed purpose which
the Prayer-book was designed to serve when read as part
of the preface to a volume which has become the excuse
of a wider diversity than it superseded. The startling

differences in the conduct of public worship perplex and distress the people, and wonderfully facilitate the task of the emissaries of the Church of Rome. My Lord, I submit that the recovery of the public confidence is a matter of extreme and urgent importance; and I suggest that this must necessitate more frankness and less individualism on the part of the clergy. The disloyal section, whatever be its numbers or importance, seems to me wholly out of place within the National Church, which would be strengthened by its secession.

III. If the Church of England is to remain an Established Church it can only be on condition that the clergy respect the National Conscience.

A witty Frenchman called the Bible and the Sunday the two English Sacraments, and there is this amount of truth in the dictum, that English Religion has fastened with extraordinary tenacity on the Supremacy of Scripture and the Sanctity of the Lord's Day. Now these are certainly not the whole of Christianity, but so far as they go they are true and valuable. It would seem the wisdom of the Church to jealously guard every sound element in the national life, and so to fashion her own teaching as to fit it on to whatever religious convictions, not actually false, the people possess. This would be the course of wisdom, and not less that of charity: unhappily it is not the course adopted by many of the English clergy. The Sabbatarian tradition, which is the abiding legacy of Calvinism and indicates with unerring decision the actual extent of its influence, has undoubtedly run into intolerable excesses of narrowness and absurdity. I remember some years ago when I opened my Vicarage garden for the use of the parishioners on Sunday afternoons, and, through the ready helpfulness of some of them, was able to provide a very creditable brass band, I received some amazing protests. One anonymous correspondent writing

from a sea-side town, which I will refrain from naming,
assured me with Apocalyptic wealth of imagery that I
" was dancing to hell with my people at my heels " !   I
am the last person in the world to assume the champion-
ship of Sabbatarian fanaticism : nevertheless, I cannot
shut my eyes to the fact that a section of the High Church
clergy is provoking a genuine moral revolt among many
godly Churchmen by its ostentatious indifference to the
sanctity of the " Lord's Day." Still more serious is the
practical contempt of the Bible which prevails in the same
quarters.   I say *practical* contempt, for theoretically there
are no signs of any such temper.   Again, I admit frankly
that respect for the Bible has very generally taken
grotesque and fanatical forms, which not unnaturally
provoke resentment and even scorn.   Yet, in the main,
who can deny that the veneration for the Scriptures is a
sound and genuinely Catholic sentiment ?   It is too plain
to be denied that the place once held in personal religion
by the regular reading of the Bible is no longer maintained.
The High Church system of replacing Mattins by Choral
Celebrations tends in the same direction.   The execrable
habit of gabbling or monotoning the Lessons goes far to
neutralize their value : and the great multiplication of
devotional books, some pernicious, many mawkish, most
superfluous, tends to crowd out the sacred volume.   The
practical neglect of the Bible is the historic condition of
ecclesiastical corruption, and I cannot conceal the real
anxiety I feel at the possible reaction on our whole Church
life of the rapidly increasing ignorance of Scripture which
I observe.   Professor Beyschlag, in the American Journal
of Theology (July, 1898), relates that in the Vatican
Council ecclesiastical indifference to the Scriptures had
reached the length of discussing the proposed doctrine
without reference to the sacred text.   " A Bible by which
" to test the new dogma seems not to have been at hand,

" for Bishop Dupanloup borrowed one of the Protestant " chaplain of the German legation." Clerical contempt of the Bible has been very prominent and aggressive in the recent controversies about religious teaching in elementary schools. I have always held and urged the insufficiency of mere Bible reading, and I do not wish to be understood as in any way receding from that belief : but to think that Bible reading is insufficient is one thing, to deride and denounce it is quite another ; and that the latter has but too often been the course adopted by the clergy is, I think, unquestionable. The general conscience, I believe, is very hostile to merely " secular " education ; and the clergy might be really supported by the moral conviction of the nation as a whole when they fight for definite Christian teaching in the schools. It is a sad misfortune that they should forfeit the political advantages of their position by provoking, often quite unpardonably, the Bible-venerating sentiment of the people.

My Lord, I cannot describe under any less severe description than that of gratuitous offence to the average conscience of Englishmen the practice, but too common, of selecting the most irritating and mis-leading language in which to discuss religious questions. I will confine myself to two examples which are ready to my hand. What excuse is there for flaunting in the face of an apprehensive public the long-discarded Roman term for Holy Communion ? Your Lordship at Bradford was careful to explain that the members of the English Church Union " believe the Holy Eucharist, whether it be more " commonly called 'the Divine Liturgy,' as in the East, " or 'the Mass,' as in the West, or 'the Holy Communion' " as amongst ourselves, to be one and the same service." I confess, my Lord, that this does not seem to me a very serviceable declaration. No sane man disputes what you say. The " Mass " claims to be the Sacrament which

Christ instituted, and so does the English Communion,
and so does the sectarian "bread-breaking." All claim
the same character; but, none the less, they are not the
same. When the average Englishman repudiates the
"Mass" and the "bread-breaking," he is not denying
that both, equally with the "Holy Communion," are
representative of the original institution; he is only
repudiating the specific and distinguishing character of
those particular representations; in the one case, the
transubstantiation-dogma and the materialized conception
of sacrifice which it involves; in the other case, the absence
of the ordained Minister, and even of the traditional
formula of consecration, and the disbelief in sacramental
grace. Is it reasonable to expect that English people
should take kindly to a term which is never used in the
public services of the Church, which is only once men-
tioned in the Prayer-book, and then contemptuously,
which is repudiated by most of the venerated "Fathers"
of the Reformed Church, which has been totally disused
in England for centuries, which is characteristic of the
Roman Church, and, finally, which is, apart from its
associations, wholly unmeaning? What conceivable
advantage to religion can be set against the certain
irritation and mistake? English clergy do not want,
or ought not to want, to make their congregations
suppose that the Roman Mass and the English Communion are *in this sense* one, that the characteristic
sacramental doctrine of the one Church is identical
with that of the other. The abolition of the term
from the formularies of the Reformed Church declared
a fact that certainly needs assertion to-day, as much as
ever, and it is really reckless on the part of any clergyman
to provoke resentment or misunderstanding, or both, by
borrowing the Roman name for the Holy Sacrament.

Again, what good purpose is served by continually

speaking of "Protestantism" and "Anglicanism" with
a contempt which at once perplexes and exasperates
the minds of average Englishmen? I adduce as an
example the language used at Bradford in your Lordship's presence by the well-known vicar of S. Augustine's,
Stepney, on which Sir William Harcourt naturally fastened
when he sought to sustain the charge of intractable disloyalty against the High Church party. I retain the notes
of applause, because they indicate how completely the
numerous assembly of members of E. C. U. identified
itself with the speaker's views :—

"Sometimes, you know, we hear of the distinctive
"doctrines of the Church of England. (Laughter.)
"Has the Church of England got any distinctive
"doctrines? If she had any distinctive doctrines she
"would be a sect, and not a portion of the Holy
"Catholic Church. (Loud cheers.) I am not the least
"surprised the Protestants are getting exceedingly anxious.
"I have been in East London about fifteen years, and can
"say that there has been a very marked change in the
"aspect of the Churches there in that time. . . . A few
"words to our friends who call themselves Anglicans.
"I was an Anglican once myself. (Laughter.) Indeed
"I was a Protestant once myself. (Renewed laughter.)
"Why, Catholics are fighting your battle; that is what I
"have to say to Anglicans. The Protestants hate your
"ways as much as ours, only it is much easier to fight us
"than you. You have got your choral services, coloured
"stoles and vestments, and the like, and, observe this, all
"that these things mean. How is it you have got them?
"Because Father Mackonochie stood firm at S. Alban's,
"Holborn. (Tremendous cheering.)"

My Lord, I read this indecent and inflammatory language
with a feeling almost of despair. But a few hours elapsed
between your approving audience of Mr. Wilson's speech,

and your proposal of a Conference to restore peace. My
Lord, can you seriously hope that any Conference can
exorcise from English minds the alarm and suspicion
which is provoked in them by Mr. Wilson's words ? I
have read them very carefully, and I think I can dimly
guess in them a meaning which is not so offensive as that
which they certainly convey; but that is not now my
point. Whatever their meaning, and I will assume it to
be compatible with loyalty to the Anglican Church, is it
possible to exaggerate the reckless uncharity of the words ?
What wanton offence it must give to feelings and beliefs
which are legitimate, reasonable, and sincere !

Of course I know, and up to a certain point I sympathize
with, the desire to bring back into the general usage of
English Churchmen that venerable and noble name
"Catholic," which the Prayer-book constantly adopts,
and which, to the educated and thoughtful Christian,
carries such a freight of Christian traditions. I know, and
I deprecate the obvious misconceptions which commonly
underlie the use of the word "Protestant"; and I entirely
approve all courteous and reasonable means for bringing
more accurate ideas into current religious language. But
how can I help repudiating with all my heart this reckless
and abusive denunciation of a name which is everywhere
in English literature a synonym for truth and freedom,
which stands for nothing less in the Archives of mankind,
which was habitually adopted by the honoured "Fathers"
of the English Church ? What a gulf parts Mr. Wilson's
rhetoric from Bishop Cosin's grave and religious language.

" But in what part of the world soever any Churches are
" extant, bearing the Name of Christ, and professing the
" true Catholic Faith and religion, worshipping and calling
" upon God, the Father, the Son, and the Holy Ghost,
" with one heart and voice, if any where I be now hindered
" actually to be joined with them, either by distance of

" countries, or variance amongst men, or by any other let
" whatsoever, yet always in my mind and affection I join
" and unite with them ; *which I desire to be chiefly understood*
" *of Protestants*, and the best reformed Churches : for,
" where the foundations are safe, we may allow, and there-
" fore most friendly, quietly, and peaceably suffer, in those
" Churches where we have not authority, a diversity, as
" of opinion, so of ceremonies, about things which do but
" adhere to the foundations, and are neither necessary or
" repugnant to the practice of the universal Church"
(Works, vol. iv., p. 527).

My Lord, if Mr. Wilson's Bradford speech stood
alone, I should certainly not have adduced it in this
Letter, but I know but too well that it is representative of
a widely extended clerical habit. The conscience of the
ordinary Englishman revolts against these diatribes against
Protestantism, and justly. No Church can afford to
ignore the general conscience. I need not remind your
Lordship how opposed such an attitude is to the teaching
of Christianity. The supercilious, contemptuous tone in
which the " Protestant " or the " mere Anglican " are
referred to in Ritualist circles seems the very counterpart
of that scornful " knowledge " which disregarded " weaker
brethren," and earned the solemn censure of the great
Apostle. " Let us not therefore judge one another any
" more : but judge ye this rather, that no man put a
" stumbling-block in his brother's way, or an occasion of
" falling. . . . Let not then your good be evil spoken of :
" for the kingdom of God is not eating or drinking, but
" righteousness and peace and joy in the Holy Ghost. For
" he that herein serveth Christ is well-pleasing to God, and
" approved of men. So then let us follow after things which
" make for peace, and things whereby we may edify one
" another " (Romans xv. 13, 17-19).

My Lord, I am not unconscious of the risks to which

my present argument is exposed. It is an easy task to sweep aside as trivial, or exaggerated, or unfair, any of the instances which I adduce as illustrating the clerical contempt of the national conscience, which, I am contending, must be restrained if the present legal Establishment of Religion is to be preserved. The cumulative effect of acts in themselves trivial can be very great, and this is the case before us. The attitude of mind revealed in Mr. Wilson's speech at Bradford finds expression in a thousand forms, the general result of which is to isolate the clergy from the sympathy and confidence of good and religious people, and to build up between the Church and the conscience of the Nation a wall of partition.

The practical mischiefs, which flow from the deep and (I at least cannot honestly deny) not unfounded suspicion of the clergy which has been thus built up in the popular mind are very great. The difficulties of reform in certain directions are enormously increased. I will give but a single example. Reservation for the Sick is, as your Lordship is wont to insist, a primitive practice ; it is also intrinsically reasonable, for the extreme weakness of very ill or dying persons, makes even a shortened Service extremely burdensome ; but, *pace* your Lordship, it is by the Law of the English Church forbidden as we have been again reminded by the Archbishop. What is the real difficulty about getting the law altered ? What is the real reason of the unanimous decision of the English Bishops (for nothing less seems behind the impressive unanimity of their Lordships' declarations on the subject), to suppress the practice ? It is nothing else than the profound distrust of the clergy which both the general public and the Bishops feel ; the former, led by a vague but strong instinct, the latter, guided by actual knowledge of the dominant tendencies in the Church, unite in suspecting that the liberty which is demanded in the interest

of the sick, would certainly be used in the interest of
liturgical developments borrowed from contemporary
Romanism, which are not only grossly materialistic in
themselves, but are also plainly opposed to the spirit and
the letter of the Prayer-book. Who can say that in this
particular this suspicion is unjust, or unreasonable ? Personally, I applaud the practice of reservation, and, on
grounds of practical convenience, I desire its restoration,
but, if such restoration is to bring into the Churches the
Roman " Benediction," and processions of the " Host,"
and such developments of debased Sacramentalism, then
I prefer the existing prohibition. And my own knowledge
of the London Churches, which, of course, is necessarily
limited, makes me quite ready to believe that such results
are highly probable.

IV. If the Church of England is to remain an Established Church, it can only be on condition that certain
evident and exasperating abuses are removed.

No observer of the recent course of ecclesiastical politics
can fail to be impressed by the rapid advance of the agitation inaugurated and maintained by the Church Reform
League. Into the merits of the particular proposals
advanced by the League I shall not here enter. It must
suffice to say that, though I cordially sympathize with
the idea of Reform, and hold very strongly that the
Establishment itself is endangered by the continuance of
certain abuses which weigh heavily on the popular conscience and do plainly run counter to the popular interest,
yet that I cannot so far reconcile myself to the avowed
ideals of the Church Reform League as to become a
member of that Association. Here I am only concerned
to point out that the removal of abuses is a condition of
the Establishment which must be faced. Parliament acts
slowly, and with obvious difficulty; but it is the only
adequate instrument of Church Reform which we possess,

and, therefore, we should not be too ready to denounce its defects. Parliament, on the whole, has not deserved ill of the Church of England. Even the ill-starred Public Worship Regulation Act was mitigated by an Episcopal veto, which in the sequel has deprived it of all effect; and in justice to the State it must always be remembered that that Act was passed in deference to the avowed wishes of the vast majority of English Churchmen. Parliament conferred an immense benefit on the Church when, in the teeth of clerical clamour, it constituted the Ecclesiastical Commission for the better administration and distribution of ecclesiastical property, and passed the Tithe Commutation Act. The recent Discipline and Patronage Acts have certainly been of great service, and I see no reason why all necessary practical Reforms should not be obtained from Parliament, if a reasonable temper of conciliation and compromise replace in Churchmen the intractable and contemptuous attitude which is now so common. Surely it ought to be possible to discuss practical questions in a practical spirit. Why must everything be treated in connection with irrelevant and exasperating beliefs, which may be lawful enough for the guidance of individuals, but cannot be usefully advanced in a practical discussion?

Here, my Lord, I may well bring my letter to a conclusion, for, if in what I have already said my meaning has not been made clear, I cannot hope to remedy the fault by protracting my argument. Your Lordship must not resent a personal appeal; it is the consequence of an influence unique in character and in extent that you should be held greatly responsible for the course of action which the High Church Party elects to follow at this juncture. I have tried without success to recall a parallel in our Ecclesiastical History to the position which you have won for yourself in the Church of England. That a layman should wield so ample an authority over thousands of the English clergy must be allowed to constitute an impressive evidence of the respect which your Lordship's high and chivalrous character, transparent sincerity, and obvious courage have inspired. With that respect, I beg to associate myself unreservedly, in spite of the fact that I have never acquiesced in the projects, or endorsed the ideals which, under your Lordship's influence, the High Church Party has of late years pursued and made its own.

It is with the High Church Party that the decision rests on the great issue whether or not the Church of England shall remain, in the historic sense of the phrase, the National Church. The Low Church Party may be, and I am honestly bound to say that I think it is, guilty of larger and more fundamental departures from the spirit and letter of the Prayer-book than its rival, but those departures have little political effect because they coincide with the general sentiment of the Nation, and command the sympathy of the Nonconformist bodies. Moreover, the Low Church Party is evidently yielding, slowly, perhaps, but apparently, to the influence of the wider culture of modern life, and the silent formative force of the Formularies. The fanatical Anti-Popery sentiment which swayed the Party a generation ago is now largely extinct, and among the younger Evangelicals there is a deep and growing appreciation of the Catholic tone and teaching of the Prayer-book. I would without anxiety leave the members of that Party to the education of their circumstances as members of a Church which believes and worships as the Prayer-book provides. This is my explanation, and I hope also my sufficient excuse for leaving out of count, when the question of Establishment is at stake, that numerous, zealous, and powerful section of the National Church.

My Lord, you have publicly avowed yourself on many

occasions the opponent of the policy of the Liberation Society ; I appeal to you very earnestly to consider whether you are not indirectly and unintentionally contributing to the very disaster you deprecate and denounce. Your Lordship spoke with generous rhetoric of the pride of Englishmen in " the ancient Church of this land " : you said, and not untruly, that " they love her, and, far from " wishing to degrade her, or to rob her, they desire " nothing so much as to see her once more the joy and " praise of the whole earth." Yes, my Lord, that is true, only do not make the fatal mistake of crediting the English people with an antiquarian or transcendental conception of the Church. They are the most practical people in the world, the least governed by sentiment and emotion. They see nothing glorious or worthy in a Church which disowns its birthright, which proclaims that it has no distinctive principles, no rightful authority, which lives in the shadowy past, or guides its hesitating course by a parasitic imitation of foreign models. The Church which Englishmen will rejoice in and exult to possess, which they will rally to and champion against domestic treason and external attack, is that which commands the homage of their conscience, and wins, by self-sacrificing labour, the affection of their hearts. Your Lordship is too fond of the past, and, as is but too often the case with lovers, you clothe the object of your affection with the qualities you would yourself most desire to see in it. Even in the ardent words I have quoted this note of imaginative archaism is audible. The English Church is "*once more*" to become " the joy and praise of the whole earth." Pray tell us, my Lord, when was that golden age ? You could hardly refer to the primitive conversion in the sixth and seventh centuries, or to the disastrous trials of the ninth, or the degraded secularism of the tenth and eleventh, or the brutal feudalism of the twelfth, or the extraordinary

oppression of the thirteenth, or the profound debasement
of the fourteenth and fifteenth, or the violent revolution of
the sixteenth. Your Lordship's words earlier in the
speech preclude the later period. What is the historic
fact on which you rear the fabric of your ecclesiastical
ideal? And by what right do you credit to the general
body of Englishmen your own imaginative devotion? Do
not misunderstand me, my Lord, I yield to no man in my
love of the National Church: her history is my favourite
study; her interest my constant anxiety: to bear her
ministry is my greatest honour. I believe in the National
Church as the most beneficent of the National Institutions;
every instinct of patriotism is outraged by the proposal to
degrade and pillage her : but this is not the deepest basis
of my loyalty. The National Church commends itself to
my conscience and reason as the most faithful representative now existing in the world of that Divine Society
which the Apostles planted, and which the primitive
martyrs watered with their blood. I look back with
reverent gratitude on her unexampled history : I look
round with solemn apprehension on her unique oppor-
tunities ; I look forward with exultation to her splendid
possibilities. I can see her defects. They are, indeed,
like the faults of the English people, very much on the
surface. She corresponds to no preconceived theory of
what a Church should be. Logic and symmetry are
singularly absent from her system. She does not strike
the imagination with the pomp of Rome, or the more
archaic magnificence of the East. But she appeals more
successfully than either to the conscience and the intellect
of a just and liberty-loving people. She reflects the
virtues and the faults of the English race, on which she
has stamped indelibly her own distinctive image. The
very aspect of the country certifies the modest, yet effec-
tual character of the National religion. Everywhere, in

obscure and remote hamlets not less than in thriving
country towns and in populous cities, there rise parish
Churches, which amaze the visitor by their solidity, or
entrance him by their sober beauty : but our Cathedrals,
when compared with the magnificence of the Continental
Churches, are, with few exceptions, modest to the verge
of meanness. Abroad it is otherwise : the general aspect
of the Churches is cheap and tawdry, but nothing can
exceed the mingled splendour and solemnity of the
Cathedrals.

English Christianity eschews the striking effects of
which Continental religion is prodigal, but it is more
thorough and robust, and perhaps covers a larger area of
the national life. Even the failures of the National
Church are not wholly without redeeming features. She
has not bound up Christianity so closely with her own
dogmas and claims as to leave the outraged conscience
no choice between accepting the latter or abandoning the
former. Her rebels go forth from her fellowship with no
purpose of that profounder treason which on the Con-
tinent marks the revolting Catholic. The Nonconformist
communities have therefore been ministerial to that great
purpose of evangelizing the English race which, it might
have been supposed, their secession would have fatally
impeded. I confess that the modesty of the National
Church, her reluctance to press her claims, her willingness
to recognize the activities of the Eternal Spirit in other
communions, seems to me no mean evidence of her
genuinely Apostolic character. She might summarize her
experiences and confess her inmost mind in the words of
that great Apostle who, perhaps, more than any other
governs her thought. "Now I would have you know,
" brethren, that the things which happened unto me have
" fallen out rather unto the progress of the Gospel ; so
" that my bonds became manifest in Christ throughout

" the whole Prætorian guard, and to all the rest; and
" that most of the brethren in the Lord, being confident
" through my bonds, are more abundantly bold to speak
" the word of God without fear. Some indeed preach
" Christ even of envy and strife; and some also of good
" will; the one do it of love, knowing that I am set for
" the defence of the Gospel; but the other proclaim
" Christ of faction, not sincerely, thinking to raise up
" affliction for me in my bonds. What then? only that
" in every way, whether in pretence or in truth, Christ is
" proclaimed; and therein I rejoice, yea, and will rejoice "
(Phil. i. 12-18).

My Lord, I appeal to you whether the points at issue
can justify destroying the National Church; or (if you
resent that absolute and terrible phrase, which yet I
cannot think excessive) of depriving the Church of England
of the splendid vantage-ground for her spiritual work
which her legal Establishment provides? It is with a
certain melancholy amazement that I observe men taking
up an intractable attitude on such trivialities as the ritual
use of incense and the legality of reservation. Oh, my
Lord, let us clear our minds of cant. What do these or
any similar ceremonies count for in the scales of reality?
Even more considerable contentions therein weighed seem
petty enough. Your Lordship will brand as heretics those
(among whom I must count myself) who *in the interest of
Trinitarian Belief* would relegate the Athanasian Creed to
an Appendix of the Prayer-book, yet the effect of that
proposal is already secured wherever High Churchmen
have succeeded in substituting a Choral Celebration of
Holy Communion for Morning Prayer. Why fight for
the shadow, when you have already surrendered the
substance?

English public opinion is very tolerant, and it grows
more tolerant daily. Erastianism in the old sense is no

longer a spiritual danger, the real peril lies in the opposite direction. There is a disposition among the average laity to make large allowance for the practical difficulties of the clergy. I am sure that the self-suppression of the High Church party would not be misunderstood. I believe all generous and religious men would receive with intense satisfaction the prospect of an escape from the present crisis. A declaration from your Lordship frankly accepting the Archbishop's recent charge as broadly defining the position of the National Church, and avowing your belief that within the lines of that position so defined, the High Church party can and ought to work, would be altogether worthy of your Lordship's loyal and manly character, and infinitely acceptable to the great mass of English Churchmen. Short of such acceptance by both contending parties I can see no reasonable prospect of any escape from the ruinous disaster to religion involved in the destruction of the National Status of the Church of England, and her impoverishment by the loss of the ancient ecclesiastical endowments.

> I have the honour to be,
>
> My Lord,
>
> Your obedient servant,
>
> H. HENSLEY HENSON.

The Right Honourable
The Viscount Halifax.